Ossian Herbert Lang

Rousseau and his Émile

Ossian Herbert Lang

Rousseau and his Émile

ISBN/EAN: 9783337034924

Printed in Europe, USA, Canada, Australia, Japan

Cover: Foto ©Andreas Hilbeck / pixelio.de

More available books at **www.hansebooks.com**

ROUSSEAU AND HIS "ÉMILE."

BY

OSSIAN H. LANG,

AUTHOR OF "COMENIUS," "BASEDOW," "GREAT TEACHERS OF
FOUR CENTURIES," ETC.

NEW YORK AND CHICAGO:

E. L. KELLOGG & CO.

1903

rise in our own country after the Revolution, Rousseau ideas were the foremost among the dominant forces.

This in itself should induce the student of educati to inquire who Rousseau was, what his ideas on educ tion were, and why they produced so wonderful effect on the world. But there is another far mc potent reason. Rousseau's "Émile" is a master-wo of child-study. The educator who reads it to get he in this most difficult of his tasks, the investigation of t nature of children, their needs, desires, whims, in she their whole physical and psychical constitution, w derive more real, practical benefit from it than he wou from hundreds of other volumes bearing on this subjec

Every educator, parents as well as teachers, ought study it with this object in view. But it requires ca tion and discrimination to read it rightly. It contai many errors, much that is impossible, much that absurd. The student would lose himself in the labyrin of thought if he should enter it unprepared.

The primary aim of this monograph is to prese merely the fundamental educational ideas of Rousse in a clear and simple manner, to point out their ped gogic value, to show their effect on modern educatio and to give a reasonable amount of information regar ing his life and such of his works as are necessary to known to understand his pedagogic theory. The di cussions of the foundation principles are of course i tended rather as helpful suggestions than final decisior Here the object has been to indicate fundamental erro and thereby to assist the student to prepare himse thoroughly for the reading the "Émile."

JEAN JACQUES ROUSSEAU.

Early Education.—Jean Jacques Rousseau was born in Geneva, June 28, 1712. His birth caused the death of his mother. His father, a poor watchmaker,* taught him to read, and then, in order to provide plenty of practice and at the same time to develop his extraordinarily acute talents, read *novels* and *romances* with him. This sort of reading had a powerful effect on his imagination, that source of his glory and his misery, but they over-excited it and developed sensuality to such an extent that he remained the slave of his passions and sensuous desires ever after and never reached that harmony, constancy, and determination in thought and action which we call character.

At the age of seven he received a number of more substantial books from the library of his grandfather, among them the works of Plutarch, which he soon preferred to all others. Examples of great courage and self-denial impressed him deeply. He loved to imagine

---

* Voltaire frequently referred to Rousseau as *garçon d'horloger* —watchmaker-boy.

himself into the men and times of which he read. One day while relating at table the story of Scævola, he frightened his father by holding out his hand over the fire to illustrate the memorable deed of his hero.

At eight, Rousseau lost his father, who, owing to some difficulties, suddenly left Geneva never to return. This marked the beginning of his restless, adventurous life that earned him the name, "Bohemian of the eighteenth century."

Roamings.—At fourteen he was put to work in an engraver's shop, but disliked the trade and ran away. After many aimless wanderings and escapades, he found a temporary home in the house of a Madame de Warens. This young, intelligent, and wealthy, but extremely sensuous woman engaged him as a servant at first, but soon felt so great an interest in him that she had him educated and became a mistress to him. Rousseau took up Latin, the Port Royal logic, mathematics, drawing, music, and botany, prepared medicaments, and studied the works of Montaigne, Descartes, Malebranche, Locke, Leibnitz, probably also Rabelais and Rollin, and other philosophers. Losing Madame de Warens' favor, he went to Lyons and was engaged as tutor for the two boys of the Grand Prévôt de Mably.

Private Tutor.—Rousseau was not at all qualified to educate children. He possessed considerable knowledge, took a lively interest in his work, and was industrious and energetic in its performance, but he lacked prudence and was much too impatient and wrathy to make a success of it. He employed only three means, viz., appealing to the emotions of his pupils, reasoning, and wrath. "As long as everything went smoothly," he wrote, "and I saw that I accomplished something, I was an angel, but I was the very devil if anything went wrong. If my pupils did not understand me, I grew excited; if they were unruly, I felt like killing them then and there. That certainly was not the way to make them learned and wise."

Sends his Children to a Foundlings' Asylum.—In 1741 Rousseau went to Paris. He gained a livelihood by copying music and writing operettas and comedies.*

He united himself informally with Thérèse le Vasseur, a pretty, industrious, and warm-hearted, but extremely ignorant woman, who had been a bar-maid in Orleans, vowing never to leave her, but also—never to marry her. Five children were born. Deaf to the protestations and imploring appeals of the unfortunate mother, Rousseau turned them all over to a foundlings' asylum, and even refused to take out papers of identification. His only excuse for this cruel and inhuman act was that he did not want to have them grow up in the foul atmosphere of his domestic life.†

---

* He had invented an ingenious system of musical notation by means of figures, which he placed before the Academy, in 1742. But instead of expected applause he received merely a moderate praise. His opera "Les Muses Gallantes" met with greater favor.

† An allusion to the neglect of his parental duties is probably made in the following passage from the "Émile." "I predict," he writes, "to any one who has natural feeling and neglects these sacred duties,—that he will long shed bitter tears over that fault, and that for those tears he will find no consolation."

Joins the Encyclopédistes.—He held for some time the
post of secretary to the ambassador to Venice. On his
return to Paris he got into the society of the celebrated
*Encyclopédistes,** was for a time an enthusiastic mem-
ber of this materialistic circle and contributed to the
encyclopedic work by writing the dictionary of music
and several minor articles.

Wins Fame by Denouncing Civilized Life.—In 1749
the Academy of Dijon offered a prize for the best essay
on the question, " Has the reconstruction of the sciences
and arts contributed to the purification of morals?"
Rousseau won the prize. He treated the subject negatively, at the advice of Diderot it seems, and tried to
prove that the progress of civilization had corrupted the
morals of mankind. Rome, he argued, was better in
its infancy than later when she had conquered the
world: science and art had degenerated the race.

The discourse caused a sensation in the literary world.

Rousseau followed up his success by publishing (1753)
another essay, on "The Origin of Inequality among
Men," in which he declared: "If nature has designed us

---

* The *Encyclopédistes,* so called because they published an en-
cyclopedia of arts and sciences, were French freethinkers, who,
starting out from a belief in a Supreme Being (*deism*), at length
" inverted Bolingbroke's plan and instead of 'patronizing Providence' did directly the opposite " and sought their salvation in
the rankest atheism. They hurled defiance at all religion, denied
the existence of spiritual life, and explained that the soul was
merely a sort of gaseous fluid of the body (*extreme materialism*).
Diderot and d'Alembert were the most celebrated of the *Encyclopédistes.*

to be healthy, I almost venture to assert that the reflec-
tive state is unnatural, and that the man who meditates
is a depraved animal." He compared the savage with the
civilized man, and decided in favor of the former. Inequality with all the demoralizing influences that have
flown to it, he declared, originated the moment that an
individual fenced in a piece of land and dared to say,
"this land belongs to me," and found people foolish
enough to believe him. The man who undertook this
was the founder of civic society. There would have
been no wars and crimes, no misery and terror, if he
had met with opposition. Society created the State,
and this led to the institution of political government.
The dangerous power of legislation and administration
in public affairs was placed in the hands of a few who
became the rulers of the people. The first step marked
the division between wealth and poverty; the second,
between power and weakness; the third, between master
and servant. Innocence, simplicity, liberty, equality,
and all the other blessings that mankind enjoyed in its
infancy were thereby destroyed. The original generation roamed through the forests, slept in the open air,
left its parents as soon as it could shift for itself, and
knew nothing of the barriers of civilization that have
shut out innocent happiness and contentment. The
original state of man, the *natural man*, was Rousseau's
ideal. "Come into the forests," he urged, "and become
men!"*

---

* The witty Voltaire, whom Rousseau had sent a copy of this
work, wrote: "I have received your new book against the
human race, and thank you for it. You will find favor with

Enjoys both Popularity and Prosperity.—Rousseau had become famous. France, Germany, and England listened with interest to his eloquent eulogy of the primitive state of man. His success brought him many offers of favor, but he refused them all. He preferred to remain independent, and to live in accordance with the democratic principles that were embodied in his epoch-making essays. He earned his livelihood as " laborer " by copying music and writing operettas.

In 1754 he published a dissertation on the comparative merits of French and Italian music, in which he assailed the former and declared that the singing in France was nothing better than a slight modification of the barking of dogs. The French were then, as they are to-day and have been at all times, very touchy on that point, and Rousseau's imprudent and hyperbolic

those for whom it is intended, but will not make them better. One could not choose more glaring colors to paint the horrors of society from which our ignorance and weakness promise themselves so many delights. Never has any one employed so much genius to make us, if possible, to beasts. When one reads your book he is seized at once with the desire to walk on all-fours. But as I have lost that habit some sixty-odd years ago, I feel to my sorrow that I am unable to begin it anew, and gladly leave this natural way to those who are more worthy to follow it than you and I. Moreover, I find it impossible to embark for Canada to live among the savages : firstly, because the ailments which I have been condemned to suffer would necessitate the services of a European physician ; and secondly, because they have war over there just now, and because the example of our nations has made them almost as bad as we ourselves are. I have to be content to stay here in your vicinity and live as peaceable savage ;" etc.

criticism had invited the hatred of all Paris upon his head. He fled and sought refuge in his native country.

At Geneva * he intended to make his permanent home, but gave up his resolution when he heard that his literary rival, Voltaire, whose sarcasm he feared, lived in the vicinity of the town, at Fernei, and departed again for France.

Writes "La Nouvelle Héloïse."—One of his admirers, a Madame d'Épinay, had caused to be built for him a fine residence in the park of La Chevrette, in the romantic valley of Montmorency, near Paris. In this hermitage, as Rousseau loved to call the place, he wrote "La Nouvelle Héloïse." This work was intended to make his leading thoughts on naturalism popular and to instill them in social life. The narrative part of the work was apparently an overt attack on the ethics of family relation. His glowing and enchanting rhetoric made the delusive phantom of free, natural love so seductive that it was apt to corrupt the better judgment of the reader through the siren-appeal to his weakness, his emotions and passions. But the author did not seek to destroy family life, as some have imagined; he came to reform it. His beautiful description of the home circle, where love reigns supreme, could not but have a beneficent influence.

In this romance Rousseau showed himself as poet. The charming descriptions of the beauties of nature that

---

* He had turned Catholic owing mainly to the influence of Madame de Warens. At Geneva he rejoined the Reformed Church, thereby regained his citizenship, and from that time styled himself *Citoyen de Genève.*

he had artfully knitted into the work to kindle in the hearts of men a love for their surroundings, and to make them look to nature for the sources of the highest and purest delights, stand to-day unrivalled, the master-work of a poetic genius. It is this part that Humboldt referred to when he called the " Héloïse " the most exquisite work on the grandeur of nature. The " Heloïse " revealed the ideals that Rousseau cherished, the confessions of his passionate soul, encased by his master-hand in beautiful diction that would bear the reader aloft to a higher goal of life.

Completes the Chain of Epoch-making Writings.—In the winter of 1757, after a quarrel with his benefactress, Rousseau suddenly left the hermitage and went to Montmorency, where he lived for five years in the castle of the Duke of Luxembourg. There he wrote the "Contrat Social"* and "Émile, ou sur l'Éducation "—the gospel of democracy and the gospel of education, as his admirers have called these master-works of French literature.

In his first essay, on the arts and sciences, Rousseau had given a general outline of his literary plan; in the second his ideas had crystallized around the central thought of naturalism (*l'homme naturel*); the three following books were designed to show the practical application of his ideas: in the "Contrat Social" with refer-

---

* In this work he sounded the battle cry of the French revolution : Liberty, equality, sovereignty of the people, the king a mandatary ! His ideal of a state was the federative republic. Robespierre and Marat learned their first lessons in civil government from his gospel of democracy.

ence to the state ; in the " Nouvelle Héloïse " with reference to the family ; and in the "Émile," this last and
greatest link in the chain of epoch-making writings, with
reference to the individual and his education. "All
these books," Rousseau said himself, "breathe the same
maxims."

Condemned by the Clergy.—The moral and religious
principles enunciated in the " Émile," particularly one
part, the "Confession of Faith of the Vicar of Savoy," called the whole clerical camp under arms. The
archbishop of Paris issued a pastoral letter, in which he
said : " Rousseau poses as a teacher of mankind in order
to defraud it, as a public warner to mislead the world,
as the oracle of the century to complete its corruption.
In a work on the inequality of the classes he has de-
graded man to a beast; in a later work (' Héloïse ') he has
instilled the poison of voluptuousness, while appearing
to condemn it ; in the Émile, he takes possession of the
first life-period of man to establish the reign of irreli-
gion." Catholics and Protestants joined to condemn the
author because of his alleged heresy and immorality,
and sought to suppress the sale of the book.

The result of the severe condemnation that fell on
the book was that there was such an enormous demand
for it that the price rose from 12 livres to 2 louis d'or.

Freethinkers Disappointed.—The ravings of the clergy
led the French freethinkers to believe that the " Émile "
was the gospel of atheism, and great was their rejoicing
for a time. But they were disappointed. The "Confession of Faith of the Vicar of Savoy " was an overt attack on the materialism of the day. Rousseau dared to

believe in Providence that was too much for the atheistic scoffers. "I endeavor to shun the two extremes, of heartless freethinking on the one hand, and blind credulity on the other," wrote the author; "I dare confess God before the philosophers, and preach humanity to persecutors."

Persecuted by his Enemies.—On June 9, 1762, the French parliament, with a view of gaining favor with the clergy and the people, condemned the "Émile" and ordered it to be burned by the public executioner in the market-place of Paris. A week later the book experienced a similar fate in Protestant Geneva. The author was to be imprisoned, but made good his escape into Switzerland. He lived for a time at Yverdon, the little town that later became so famous through the work of Pestalozzi. Banished by the government of Berne, he fled to Moitiers, Neufchatel, and thence to the isle of St. Pierre in Lake Biele. There he was for a time left unmolested in his solitude, until the persecutors found him and forced him to leave the country. Driven about from place to place by the enraged clergy of every denomination, he finally found refuge in England in the house of Hume, the philosopher. Quarrelling with his benefactor, he returned to France. He was permitted to live in the vicinity of Paris on condition that he would refrain from publishing anything of a revolutionary nature.

Writes his "Confessions."—The last days of his restless life were spent at Ermenonville, north of Paris, on the beautiful country-seat of the Marquis de Girardin. There he wrote his "Confessions." In this voluminous work, partly truth, partly fiction, he has left to the world his autobiography.

Last Days and Death.—Filled with hatred against the race for whose happiness he had labored, suffering the tortures of a diseased body and a restless mind, he lived the life of a hermit. Dressed in a strange Armenian costume, he wanted to be regarded by the outer world as a "stranger" without home and without friends. He died, suddenly, July 2, 1778, at Ermenonville.* Some believe that he took poison, others that he shot himself; but these assumptions are unwarranted.

He was buried on the same day on the poplar island of Ermenonville. His epitaph bears this inscription:

> " Here where the poplars lonely sprout rests Rousseau's body.
>   Ye hearts pure and warm,
>   The tombstone hides your friend."

On October 11, 1794, the body was exhumed and thought to the Parthenon. There he rests side by side with Voltaire. The sarcophagus bears the inscription,

> "To the Man of Nature and of Truth."

A Laconic Criticism.—Some one has judged Rousseau very tersely in these words: "Jean Jacques Rousseau was *born* at Geneva, *thought* at Paris, *wrote* at Montmorency, *plagued* and *tormented* himself everywhere. His *body* he left to Ermenonville, his *head* to Émile,

---

* The reverence of the French revolutionists for Rousseau saved Ermenonville from being burned down in the time of the Commune.

his *heart* to Julia,* and in his 'Social Contract' he be-
queathed to the world the *restlessness* of his soul."

Review of Rousseau's Life.—Rousseau was by nature
endowed with the rare gift of genius. His wonderful
imagination, the power to clothe his thoughts in beautiful and enchanting diction, the glowing enthusiasm that
charmed the age in which he lived and converted it to
the grand ideas in his writings, made him immortal.
This is the ideal Rousseau, the Rousseau whom the
world admires and honors as a classic.

How different from this is the real Rousseau, judged
by the conduct of his life! Examine him as we may,
we will not discover one trait that might be taken as
suggesting the ruling principle of his life. All is con-
tradiction. The moral maxims that he upholds in his
writings are trodden down in his conduct. He preaches
charity and hates mankind, although he starts out to
make the world happy. He insists that he who cannot
fulfil the duties of a father has no right to become
such, and sends his children to a foundling asylum.†
He condemns society for the very vices in which he
fairly wallows. He seeks friends, then turns away from
them and aims to crush them with the power of his pen,
and then, too weak to shun them, too weak to stand
alone, clings to them again for support. He wants to
lead the thoughts of mankind, and is himself most in

---

* "La Nouvelle Héloïse."

† In his "Confessions" he writes that this has often caused him
bitter remorse ; but it cannot have been very serious, for he never
took steps to get his children back, although he could have done
so with little difficulty.

need of guidance. He attempts to set up a new ideal, and has never fathomed its depth. There is hardly a vice that he has not tasted. Constantly seeking for happiness, he destroys it wherever he finds it. He has no fixed maxims to govern his will, no energy to follow those that he proclaims to be true and good: he is, in short, a man without character, at the mercy of circumstances, of a mad ambition, a slave of passions and sensous desires.

ROUSSEAU'S "ÉMILE," OR TREATISE ON EDUCATION.

How Rousseau came to Write the "Émile."—The revolution of thought that the French nation was undergoing had aroused all reflecting minds, and, as is ever the case when the ideals of society suddenly change, all eyes turned to education for the realization of the hopes of the age. Eminent writers, like Duclos, Chalotais, and Cayer, took up the pen to solve the educational problem. Anxious mothers inquired for advice to learn how to educate their children to make them happy and wise. It was in answer to the request of one of these good and thoughtful mothers, a Madame Dupin de Chenonceaux, that Rousseau wrote the "Émile." In the preface to this grand work he wrote: "My original purpose was to write only a memorandum of a few pages; but my theme led me on against my will, and that memorandum, before I realized it, became a sort of book, too large, doubtless, for what it contains, but too small for the subject which it discusses."

Hesitated about Publishing it.—When the author had completed this "last and best work," as he himself called it, he placed the manuscript before the Duchess of Luxembourg, to whom he had previously read the "Héloïse" and the "Social Contract" before publishing them, to hear her judgment concerning it. The duchess was not as favorably impressed with the work as the author had expected. But she offered to find a publisher for it.* Owing to the censor laws, the work could not be printed in France and had to be sent to Holland. It appeared in Paris in 1762. Rousseau wrote: "I hesitated a long time about publishing it; and I was often made to feel, while working at it, that the writing of a few pamphlets is not a sufficient preparation for composing a book. After vain efforts to do better, I think it my duty to publish my book just as it is, judging that it is important to turn public attention in this direction, and that, even though my ideas are perchance bad, my time will not be wholly lost if I succeed by this means in *stimulating others to produce better ones.*"

The Kernel of the Book.—The pedagogic testament of the "citizen of Geneva" is a voluminous work, nearly the size of a bible, covering about 2400 (12mo) pages. There is no attempt at a systematic arrangement of thoughts; it is, as the author says himself, "a collection of reflections and observations, *without order and almost without connection.*" Any attempt to bring order and harmony into them would prove a futile task. The

---

* He was a poor judge of men and would have reaped but little financial benefit from his writings if it had not been for his benefactress, who knew how to place them advantageously.

kernel of Rousseau's pedagogy is *education according to nature.* The child is to grow to *manhood,* to become a healthy and reasonable man, relying solely upon himself for happiness. His education is to be adapted to his gifts, powers, needs, dispositions, qualities, in short his individuality, following the order of nature, as shown in the natural development of his physical and psychical powers. Self-reliance is to be reached by promoting the pupil's self-activity in thought and action. The best education, accordingly, is that which does the least for the pupil and merely prevents corrupting influences from obstructing his natural development. In order to educate rightly, the child must be studied; for thereby we learn the way that nature has pointed out for man to follow.

The Distinctive Purpose of the Book.—" Childhood is not known," says Rousseau; " it is the study upon which I am most intent, to the end that, though my method may be chimerical and false, profit may always be derived from my observations." To turn the thoughts of educators to the child, to make him, and not the studies, the centre of educational activity, that was the purpose of Rousseau. He did not intend to give them a method that if strictly followed out would prove a panacea for all evils. That is why he wrote: " An education of a certain kind may be practicable in Switzerland, but not in France; one kind of education may be best for the middle class, and another for the nobility. The facility of execution, greater or less, depends on a thousand circumstances which it is impossible to determine save by a particular application of the method to such or such a country, or to such or such a condition. Now, all such special applications, not being essential to my subject, do not form a part of my plan." When Rousseau was told by an admirer that his son was being educated after the method of the "Émile," he said, "So much the worse for him." His plan was to describe an ideal human life and thereby to stimulate others to search for the right ways and means to realize it in education.

The Story of Émile.—Rousseau presents his ideas on education in the form of a romance. He begins with the birth of Émile, the hero of the story. To isolate him from the influence of the family and the social and political institutions of civilization, he makes him an orphan. His only companion is his tutor, who guides his education for twenty-five years and instructs him till he is married and has children of his own. When Émile reaches the years of puberty, his tutor brings about a meeting with Sophie, the young woman whom he has chosen to become his pupil's wife. (Describing Sophie, Rousseau reveals his ideas on the education of women.*) After the marriage has been decided on,

---

* His ideas on this subject are very crude, even for the age in which he lived. "Woman," he writes, "is especially constituted to please man. The whole education of women ought to be relative to men. To please them, to be useful to them, to make themselves loved and honored by them, to educate them when young, to care for them when grown, to counsel them, to console them, and to make life agreeable and sweet to them—these are the duties of women at all times, and that should be taught them from their infancy."

Émile is separated from Sophie for two years to learn to brave misfortune. He begins the study of family, social, and civic organization, and then travels with his tutor through the principal European states, to observe the genius and habits of the different nations and to become acquainted with the workings of political constitutions and the leaders of thought. At twenty-four he marries Sophie. The tutor stays with the young couple for a time and advises them as to the ways and means to make matrimonial life a heaven of bliss. Children are born, and the tutor, after having instructed them respecting their education, takes leave of his beloved pupils. It seems that the demon of destruction from whose grasp Rousseau could never free himself tortured him so that he added some years later "Émile et Sophie, ou les solitaires." In this book he tore the beautiful picture he had painted of matrimony in the "Émile" and with one stroke of his pen destroyed all the happiness he had created. Sophie proves faithless; Émile leaves her in despair, comes to Algiers and is made a slave. With this Rousseau intended to show that a man brought up after his plan could not be conquered even in the most adverse situations.

Uses up One Man to Educate Another.—Rousseau, as Herbart put it, sacrifices in theory the whole individual life of the teacher, whom he gives up to be the boy's constant companion. This education costs too dear. There is some truth in the saying that "education lasts as long as life;" but that certainly does not mean that man must be constantly guided by another. Émile has a tutor up to the age of twenty-five. Even then he has not yet reached the aim which, Rousseau says, is self-reliance; for he begs the tutor not to leave him, but to guide him on. He confesses his inability to stand on his own feet. This is one of the many examples of con-tradictory ideas in the book.

Private Education.—Rousseau believes with Locke, to whom he is indebted for many ideas, that isolated, private education is better than the social training in family and school. He himself had never experienced the blessings of an education in a well-regulated home. The schools of that time were exceedingly poor. Be-sides, he intended to describe a *natural* education, whatever that means, and to this end to isolate the pupil from the influences of civilized life. Lastly, the book was intended for a mother of the aristocratic class * who would engage a private tutor for her boy.

This isolation from social life gives rise to many con-flicting statements. Rousseau insists that in a natural education the mother is the rightful nurse of the child and the father the rightful teacher, then in describing a natural (?) education he makes the pupil an orphan and gives him a tutor who hires a nurse for the infant, although he advises, shortly before, justly and vigorously against hired nurses.

Contradictions.—Speaking of contradictions, we hardly know where to begin to point them out. The book is full of them. One might, if it were worth the trouble

---

* He writes: " The poor man has no need of an education, for his condition in life forces one upon him, and he could receive no other."

cull from it a large volume of unripe assertions, exaggerations, and most nonsensical statements. Once the author insists that all is to be sacrificed to present happiness, arguing that the pupil may never grow up to manhood; then in other paragraphs Émile is subjected to all sorts of tortures, because he will be all the better for it when grown up. Again and again Rousseau insists that education ought to be purely *negative* in childhood, and then describes an education that might be called anything but negative. He believes that the example of the educator is a most important power, and then makes his model tutor deceive Émile in order to impress some truth. On the one hand he tries to make us believe that the sciences and arts have corrupted mankind, and on the other, teaches the pupil drawing, music, mathematics, geography, history, civil government, physics, etc.

SOME GENERAL PRINCIPLES CONSIDERED.

1. *Man is born good.* The dispositions, including sensations and feelings, with which he is by nature endowed, tend spontaneously to the good. Goodness, consequently, must be life according to nature, or to what man is by nature.

This is certainly a wrong premise. Man is neither good nor bad by nature: he is *guiltless*—that is all. He is susceptible for both good and evil; for the latter, as experience shows, even more than the former, as he is naturally sensuous and selfish and has not yet the power to control his desires.

2. *Education is derived from three* **sources:** (1) *from* NATURE, (2) *from* MEN, (3) *from* THINGS. The inner development of our faculties and organs is the education of nature; the use which we learn to make of this development, that of men; the acquisition of personal experience from the objects that affect us, that of things. All these educative influences must tend to the same end. The education derived from men is the only one of which we are truly the masters; that of things depends on ourselves only in certain respects; while that of nature is entirely independent of ourselves. Since the co-operation of the three educations is necessary to attain the best results, it is to the one over which we have no control that we must direct the other two.

Rousseau takes too general a view of education. What he calls the education of nature is simply undirected natural development and does not deserve the name of education, else we might speak also of educated plants and minerals. But his principle contains a sound kernel of truth. The educator cannot make the child what he wants him to be. The environment and the experiences gained from the observation and handling of things are influences over which he has no absolute control. Hence to gain the greatest possible power over the pupil he must carefully study him, measure the quality, force, and extent of the influences other than his own on his growth and direct them to the end he aims at.

3. *Nature points out the aims of education.* According to this principle, those living in the lowest grade of savagery ought to be the best authorities as to what

aims to pursue in education, as nature, i.e., their natural impulses, is their only guide. The study of human nature reveals the laws of inner development, but not its destiny. The highest purpose of human life—and with that is given the aim of education—is determined by moral philosophy, or ethics. It has taken many hundreds of years to reach an agreement as to what should be the aim of every man. It is absurd to assume that if men should be left to themselves their impulses would tell them that they are to strive for moral strength of character. Rousseau's principle is entirely wrong.

4. *The aim of education is the natural man.* Rousseau wants to form a natural man, a *savage*, as he explains in another passage. What his conception of a *natural man* is he has shown in his essay on "The Origin of Inequality among Men" (see page 9). He holds that the state, like all other strongholds of civilization, is an unnatural institution. He ignores reality entirely, imagines himself in the time before the dawn of civilization, and builds up a utopian world of his own. Following him in this, we would have to destroy all traces of civilization, blot out the pages of history, live in forests, "every man for himself, and " etc., and then in as many thousand years as we have started back—we would be exactly where we are now. The anarchists are to-day about the only people that worship at this Rousseauian shrine.

But while we cannot agree with the idea of educating savages, we do not altogether reject the aim of education as stated by Rousseau. Here, as nearly everywhere in the " Émile," we must take the ideas as they stand, not

as the author wants them understood, but as we ourselves
explain them. Taking the proposition negatively, we
may even allow it to stand that the aim *is* the natural
man. We certainly do not want to make the children
unnatural. But our natural man is not a Fiji islander.
He is a man whose nature is fully and completely developed, strong and healthy in body and mind, a man of
character. His natural state is civilized life, into that
he is born, in that he grows up, and the greatest perfection possible in it is his highest natural state. The
trouble with the term *natural* is that it has lost significance by indiscriminate use.

While strictly adhering to the chameleon "natural
man" idea, Rousseau's book reveals on almost every page
that what is really aimed at is HAPPINESS, i.e., the least
possible evil. Everything seems to centre in this eude-
monistic principle. We in our day, theoretically at least,
believe that happiness follows of itself if the individual
has been trained to adapt himself to changing circumstances, and aim to give him the power to do it. But
even this is only a subordinate purpose of education.
The goal that we are striving for is virtue, and hence
we look upon the development of moral strength of
character as the true purpose of education.

In explaining how happiness is to be attained, Rousseau approaches the modern idea of education. He says
that it is of little consequence whether the pupil be des-
tined for the army, the church, the bar, or any other
vocation : *to live* is the trade he is to learn. He then
who knows best how to support the good and evil of
life is the best educated. He must know how to pro-

tect himself in the years of manhood, to bear the blows of destiny, to live, if need be, amid the snows of Iceland or on the burning rocks of Malta. Here Rousseau shows plainly that education should develop *self-reliance,* and enable the pupil to practically adapt himself to changing circumstances. " Keep the child dependent upon things alone," he writes, " and you will have followed the order of nature."

5. *Education must follow the order of nature.* According to the passage quoted just before, this would seem to mean : " keep the child dependent upon things alone." But the maxim implies more, and, as further explained in the " Émile," is sound. The only fault we find with it is that it is too general to suggest its deeper meaning. Rabelais, Montaigne, Bacon, Ratich, Comenius, and Locke wanted education to proceed " in accordance with the laws of nature " too, but each one gave it a different meaning. Rousseau insisted that it should be explained as " *in accordance with the laws of the natural development of man.*"

6. *Education must adapt itself to the individuality of the child.* It is one of the greatest merits of Rousseau to have established this truth forever. How earnestly he adhered to this important principle is shown on almost every page of the " Émile." He argues : Each mind has a peculiar bent, its own particular form, according to which it must be governed, and for the success of our undertaking it is necessary that it should be governed by this form and by no other. Study the individuality of the pupil carefully before you act. At first leave the germs of his character at perfect liberty

to unfold, and put no constraint whatever upon him, in
order that you may the better see him in his completeness.   In infancy, therefore, sacrifice time which you
will regain with interest at a later period.

7. *The principal condition for the success of education is that the educator knows and loves his pupil.*
This is a fundamental truth.   The teacher must study
child-nature and his pupil in particular before he can
undertake to educate him.   Rousseau would have him
be a young man—"just as young as a man can be and
be wise,"—believing that in order to secure a really solid
attachment between the child and his educator, the
difference in age should not be too great.   "Were it
possible," he writes, "I would have him a child, so
that he might become a companion to his pupil and
secure his confidence by taking part in his amusements."

8. *What are we to do ?   Much, doubtless, but chiefly
to prevent anything from being done.*   This paradox
explains itself if compared with Rousseau's conception
of the primal man.   As he believes the child to be naturally good and endowed with instincts that tend spontaneously to the good, he is best educated by simply
keeping away from him corrupting influences.   The
educator should guide him somewhat, but only very
little, and without seeming to guide him.   He must not
so much give information as to cause the child to discover for himself what he should know.

9. *Self-reliance is the fruit of self-activity in
thought and action.*   This is the golden rule in all
good teaching.   Only what the pupil has gained himself
by honest effort is really his own.   But this should not

mean that he is to be left to himself. The teacher directs the pupil's activity, and brings that within reach which is to be acquired, but he does not do things for him and give or force information upon him. Rousseau writes : "It is not proposed to teach the pupil the sciences, but to give him a taste for them, and methods for learning them, when this taste shall be better developed." He would have the pupil discover the sciences for himself. This is going to an extreme. It has taken many centuries to bring the sciences to the height which they have reached up to the present day. The pupil would consequently have to live these years of experimenting and recording of results over again. The truth that lies in Rousseau's thought is that the pupil is to be taught by observation and experiment rather than by information. The point that instruction should aim at stimulating and developing the child's taste, or interest, for the sciences instead of mere knowledge of them, is perfectly sound and forms to-day one of the fundamental principles of teaching.

WHY WE PRIZE THE "ÉMILE" AS A CLASSIC.

General Effect of the "Émile."—But after all, it is not so much what Rousseau said on education, but how he said it, that made him great. For although full of sophisms, paradoxes, and glaring contradictions, interweaving sound truths with errors and rank absurdities, the influence of "Émile" converted the world to the appreciation of an education founded on the immutable laws of nature, development of self-reliance in thought

and action, and a healthy growth of the human organ-
ism ; and thus accomplished more than any of the pedagogic works that preceded it. It certainly contained
nothing new—the thoughts it brought out were those
that Rabelais, Comenius, Montaigne, Locke, Fénelon,
Fleury, Rollin, and others had uttered long before him;
but—and herein lies the true worth of the "Émile"—
Rousseau told the truths that were to guide the education of youth better than those before him, and therefore was better listened to than they. In other words,
Rousseau's "Émile" popularized the philosophy of education that the great thinkers of ages had built up but
failed to bring home to those for whom it was intended.

What gave the Book Epoch-making Power.—Up to
the time of Rousseau the principles derived from the
nature of the studies were the guides, how to adapt the
child to the logical order of science the uppermost question, in pedagogy. The "Émile" exploded this unnatural and false principle, and founded education on a
new basis, on the study of child-life. How to adapt
education to the different stages of growth was the
"burden" of this legacy to pedagogy. Rousseau was a
master in the art of picturing childhood. He revealed
the whole physical and psychical life of children. He
showed man as nature had made him, and followed his
natural growth from the vegetative stage of infancy to
the highest human perfection in complete manhood.
The disastrous effects of substituting artificial means
for those founded on the laws of life, of perverting the
order of nature and subduing her educative influences,
were painted in glaring colors. Faults of children that

escaped the notice of educators were uncovered; on the other hand, he pointed out the narrow-mindedness of adults who looked upon childish mischief as a crime and stamped carelessness as malice. The introduction into the real, innermost life of childhood, into the natural causes of the formation of good and evil habits, formed the nucleus of the "Émile" and gave the book the epoch-making power.

Why the "Émile" Accomplished more than Previous Works on Education.—The thought that the child must be studied to educate him rightly had, like the motive of fugue, been heard again and again, since the time of Bacon in endless variations; but while the majority tried to make their improvisations over the theme conform to scientific rules and lost themselves in technicalities that could not interest their audience, Rousseau took up the motive and wove it into a charming melody that appealed to the hearts of fathers, mothers, and teachers, and gave them a taste of an ideal life. He knew the child; he had studied him as he found him in the palaces of the wealthy and in the huts of the lowly; he knew his whims, his feelings and desires—even his vices had not escaped his searching eye. He pictured him as he had found him, avoiding all generalization and systematizing of results. That struck home. Parents recognized their children in the painting, they saw the sources of their virtues and vices; the author kept within reach of their understanding and did not, like Locke for instance, demand a knowledge of abstract metaphysical laws. Thus the "Émile" became the herald of a new education; it pointed to a new, a psychological basis on which pedagogics must be built, and brought abundant material for the construction of such a foundation.

Leads to the Foundation of a New Philosophy of Education.—"Study your pupils more closely," wrote Rousseau, "for it is very certain that you do not know them; and if you read this book of mine with that purpose in view, I do not believe that it will be without profit to you." That struck home. The study of child-life received a new impulse and turned from the sterile rocks of speculation to the vast and fruitful fields of reality. Pestalozzi was inspired by this thought; he followed Rousseau to the summit of the Nebo and saw the beautiful world of new education beyond. His philosophy of education immortalized the fundamental thoughts of the "Émile." Froebel caught its spirit, and turning from the playful activities of the child to the prompting impulses within found a new paradise of childhood. Herbart heard the plea for recognition of the child's individuality and made it the keystone of his science of education. Thus Rousseau's masterly treatment of the subject of child-study led to the foundation of a new philosophy of education, one that would not force all human beings into the Procrustean bed of a scientifically constructed homunculus, but would take the child as he is, with all the incongruities and surprises of his individual nature, and adapt itself in its processes to his physical and mental capabilities. If it had been known before Rousseau that each child must be studied for himself and that physiology and psychology can give only the general laws of human growth that make the study of individualities easier and more accurate, but cannot be accepted as an equivalent substitute, it had never been made sufficiently clear and important and was certainly never acted upon. The impulse given to the study of childhood must be directly attributed to the influence of the "Émile," notwithstanding the many excellent psychological and pedagogical treatises that preceded it.

Gives the Key to the Pedagogic Treasures of the Past. —There is yet another effect that might be traced back to this source. But we must proceed cautiously to detect its import. We must also constantly bear in mind that Basedow was at work at the same time with Rousseau. While the latter laid particular stress on the study of the child, the former was reconstructing the system of education on the basis of psychological laws. Basedow, too, had made a study of the child, but, unlike Rousseau, he did not attempt to break with all the great educators that lived before his time, but sought rather to modernize their ideas so as to be in accord with the laws that his knowledge of childhood had found to be fundamental. He had given his whole life to the reconstruction of the theory and practice of education, while the author of the "Émile" had through a mere incident turned to the study of the needs of childhood. He had made a thorough study of the writings of Comenius and had embodied in his system of education the thoughts that his psychologic judgment found sound. "Comenius has pointed out the right way," he was wont to say. This constant reference to Comenius called attention to the work that for a century had been a "stone which the builders refused." What else was there left for the influence of the "Émile" to do in this direction? It could help to make Comenius' pedagogy "the headstone in the corner." And that it has done. By making the study of the child the first duty of the educator, it set up a standard by which to measure the educational theories of the past. The student felt that he must find the psychological basis of pedagogic systems to appreciate their intrinsic value. Basedow had revived the study of Comenius and had gathered the thoughts that would stand the severest test in practice; Rousseau gave the key to the right appreciation of their import. Briefly told, the "Émile" stimulated the educators to make a *critical* study of the theories of education.

Why the "Émile" Struck Home.—If we look for the secret of the wonderful effect of the "Émile," we shall find that it lies entirely in the manner in which the author presented his thoughts. There is nothing scholastic about it, no attempt at a scientific arrangement of thoughts. It is the work of an artist, a poet, full of feeling and glowing passion. Its great and distinctive purpose is made clear, not by appealing to reason, but by rousing the emotions of the reader, by alluring him into depths of error and raising him again higher and higher up to the dizzy summit of truth. Rousseau here shows himself as a master in the knowledge of human nature. No one wants to be told that he is in need of instruction and must follow the author's reasoning closely and learn from him. Yet if his judgment is taken captive by a weird and seductive style, he forgets that he is guided and follows willingly. That is the charm of Rousseau's "Émile." The generation that saw its advent had felt the pressure of dogmatic preaching too long, it shunned cold reasoning. That made the time the poets' reign. And it was the poesy of the "Émile" that could succeed where the arguments of Locke, Voltaire, and Basedow had failed. The value of the "Émile" as an educational classic is in the main of historical significance, for it started the train of thoughts that built up the modern philosophy of education. Brant's "Ship of Fools" and Rabner's "Satires" have also in their way effected a progress in education, but— and here lies the difference between the "Émile" and other epoch-making books—their mission ended with the birth of the change that they aimed at, and they are to-day studied merely for the glimpses they afford into the origin of certain upward movements in the history of pedagogics, while Rousseau's "Émile" will be read as long as there is a philosophy of education, and will ever be a source of inspiration and a guiding star to the educator who knows how to sound the value of its ideas.

Read the "Émile" as you would a Poem.—The "Émile" is a mine of pedagogic thought. But it takes a soundly-trained mind to discover the treasures it contains. The bewitching rhetoric of Rousseau is apt to mislead the unwary reader, and taking his judgment captive, tempts him to pick up gleaming but worthless metals and conceals from him the countless gems that are strewn about. An easily-influenced soul whose whole life centres in the emotions is plunged from one extreme into the other ; the subtle nihilism of the author saps the roots of innocent faith and cripples judgment and reason. On a coldly-analyzing mind, that breaks the glittering shell to find the hidden kernel, the effect is disappointing, or perhaps entirely lost. Take the witty Voltaire, for instance, whose cold and cutting sarcasm Rousseau feared more than all the attacks and persecutions from the literary yelpers of his time: he rends the beautiful painting to show that it is canvas at seventy-five sous a yard. The "Émile" must be read as one would read Longfellow's "Evangeline" or Schiller's "The Walk." We would not use the former master-work as a text-book for the study of the historical events on which it is based, nor could the latter poem serve as a substitute for a treatise on the evolution of civilization. But the light that streams out from these poems gives life to the facts of history and deepens our insight in them. So with the "Émile." It is not a text-book on pedagogics and cannot be used as such: it is a work of art, a poem. Without a previous knowledge of the fundamental laws of education, its true value cannot be appreciated; it intoxicates the judgment as Byron's "Heaven and Earth" or Schiller's "Gods of Greece" would a wavering mind. But one who has passed the elementary stage of the study of pedagogics will find it an ever-fresh source of new and inspiring thoughts to strengthen his love of childhood, his feeling of the dignity of the work of rearing children, his appreciation of the value of the laws of human growth as guiding principles in the work of education, and his insight into the truth that it is not what man knows but what he is that determines his life-efficiency.

Helps in Teaching Geography.

ANALYTICAL QUESTIONS IN GEOGRAPHY,

is the best little book of questions and answers published. Invaluable for review or to question a class. Limp cloth. Price, **25 cents.**

AUGSBURG'S EASY DRAWINGS FOR THE GEOGRA-

PHY CLASS. Here are presented over 200 simple drawings that can be placed on the blackboard by any teacher, even the one ignorant of the simplest rules. An island, an isthmus, a cape, mountain ranges, animals, plants, etc., are illustrated in profusion. Opposite each plate a lesson in geography is given that may be used in connection, and an index brings any plate sought for instantly to the eye. There is no book like it published. Quarto, tasteful cardboard cover, 40 large plates, 90 pages. Price, 50 cents ; to teachers, **40 cents** ; by mail, 5 cents extra.

KELLOGG'S GEOGRAPHY BY MAP DRAWING.

By Amos M. Kellogg. The object of this book is to encourage and aid the teacher in the effort to have his pupils draw geographical forms on the blackboard with readiness and pleasure. The book shows the teacher how to make geography the most interesting of all the studies pursued in the schools. It is profusely illustrated with outline maps. The type is large and clear and the page of good size. Limp cloth. Price, 50 cents ; to teachers, **40 cents** ; by mail 5 cents extra.

DEAN'S THE GEOGRAPHY CLASS : HOW TO INTER-

EST IT. By M. Ida Dean. How will you study Germany, or France, or Egypt, or China, so as to fix the facts in the child's mind, without effort, through his intense interest? Is not that your problem in geography? Miss Dean's book tells you how —solves the problem. Her description of "A Day in Asia," and "A Day in Egypt," makes us all wish we had been there. Awaken the interest of your pupils and parents. Fully illustrated. Limp cloth. Price, **35 cents,** postpaid.

MALTBY'S MAP MODELING IN GEOGRAPHY AND HIS-

TORY. By Dr. Albert E. Maltby, Prin. Slippery Rock State Normal School, Pa. This book is of the greatest value to teachers of Geography and History. It is literally crammed full of the most helpful suggestions, methods, devices. It considers fully the use of sand, clay, putty, paper pulp, plaster-of-paris, and other materials in map modeling ; also chalk modeling. The chapters on Home Geography are exceedingly valuable. Those who would co-ordinate Geography with Science teaching will here find much to assist them. The chapter on Nature Study will give a great deal of help. There are over one hundred illustrations, many of them being full-page. Handsomely bound in cloth. Large size. 229 pages. Price, **$1.25** ; to teachers, **$1.00** ; postage, 10 cents.

E. L. KELLOGG & CO., 61 E. 9th Street, New York.

BOOKS ON
CHILD STUDY

Hall's Contents of Children's Minds on Entering

SCHOOL. By Dr. G. STANLEY HALL. Details the results of an inquiry into a matter of much importance to primary teachers. A knowledge of what the average child already knows when he first goes to school will be a valuable guide in determining not only what to teach him but how to teach him.

This little book gives the results of careful investigations made by the writer and others to determine the amount and kind of knowledge possessed by the average child on entering school. The book opens up a valuable field of inquiry and shows how it may be carried on. It is sure to interest teachers.

All "Child Study" organizations should read this book. Dr. Hall is the acknowledged leader of the child study movement in this country.

Size, 6 3-8 x 4 1-2 inches. 56 pages. Limp cloth covers. 25 cents.

Hall's A Study of Dolls.

By Pres. G. STANLEY HALL. This is a very full account of one of the most complete and satisfactory investigations along the line of "Child Study" that have been undertaken. It is first presented in this book in a form for general circulation and must prove of the greatest value to all pursuing any study or investigation of the intellectual life of children. Child study circles will do well to make a study of this book.

Size, 7 1-4 x 5 inches. 69 pages. Limp cloth cover. 25 cents.

Hall's Story of a Sand Pile.

By G. STANLEY HALL. This extremely interesting story was published some years ago in *Scribner's Magazine* and is now for the first time made accessible to the great body of teachers. All interested in the great child study movement should read this very suggestive story. A photograph of the "Sand Pile" is given. Limp cloth. 25 cents.

Perez's First Three Years of Childhood.

By BERNARD PEREZ, Edited and translated by Alice M. Chrystie, with an introduction by James Sully.

This is the most widely known and without doubt the greatest and most valuable study of infant psychology. It is an important book for the library of the student of education. For the great body of teachers who are now interested in Child Study this is the first book to read. No teacher can intelligently study children from the age of five years who has not made some study of the psychology of earlier years.

Our edition is the handsomest published. It has a new index of value and is well printed and bound.

Size, 7 1-2 x 5 inches. 295 pages. Library cloth binding, $1.50; to teachers, $1.20; postage, 10 cents.

KELLOGG'S
TEACHERS' LIBRARY.

Seventeen volumes, uniform in size and binding, covering all sides of educational thought—History of Education, Methods of Teaching, Principles of Education, Child Study, Psychology, Manual Training, Nature Study, and School Gymnastics. Each volume is 7 1-2 x 5 inches in size, with elegant and durable cloth covers stamped in two colors and gold. Every book in this library is the best, or one of the best, of its kind; the greatest writers and thinkers on education are represented—Parker, Joseph Payne, Herbert Spencer, Page, Quick, and others; it is a collection invaluable for the thinking teacher.

1.	Parker's Talks on Pedagogics	$1.50
2.	Parker's Talks on Teaching	1.00
3.	Seeley's Common School System of Germany	1.50
4.	Bancroft's School Gymnastics	1.50
5.	Spencer's Education	1.00
6.	Page's Theory and Practice of Teaching	1.00
7.	Currie's Early Education	1.25
8.	Patridge's Quincy Methods	1.75
9.	Perez's First Three Years of Childhood	1.50
10.	Tate's Philosophy of Education	1.50
11.	Quick's Educational Reformers	1.00
12.	Noetling's Notes on the Science and Art of Education	1.00
13.	Love's Industrial Education	1.00
14.	Payne's Nature Study	1.00
15.	Shaw's National Question Book	1.00
16.	Payne's Lectures on Education	1.00
17.	Welch's Teachers' Psychology	1.25

We also publish four other Teachers' Libraries as follows:

Reading Circle Library, - 16 Vols. | Teachers' Manual Library, 25 Vols.
Teachers' Professional Library, | School Entertainment Library.
13 Vols. |

17 ▽ 718

TWO EXCELLENT
SINGING BOOKS

SONG TREASURES

Compiled by AMOS M. KELLOGG, Editor of THE TEACHERS' INSTITUTE. This little book is one of the best for school use we have ever seen.

1. Most of the 100 pieces have been selected by teachers as the ones the pupils love to sing.

2. All have a ring to them ; are easily learned.

3. Themes and words are appropriate for young people. Nature, the Flowers, the Seasons, the Home, our duties, our Creator, are entuned with beautiful music.

4. Great ideas may find an entrance into the mind thru music.

5. Many of the words have been written especially for the book.

6. The titles here given show the teacher what we mean :

Ask the Children, Beauty Everywhere, Be in Time, Cheerfulness, Christmas Bells, Days of Summer Glory, The Dearest Spot, Evening Song, Gentle Words, Going to School, Hold up the Right Hand, I Love the Merry Merry Sunshine, Kind Deeds, Over in the Meadows, Our Happy School, Scatter the Germs of the Beautiful, Time to Walk, The Jolly Workers, The Teacher's Life, Tribute to Whittier, etc., etc.

15 Cts. a copy; $1.50 a dozen. Special prices quoted on larger quantities.

BEST PRIMARY SONGS

Compiled by AMOS M. KELLOGG. This book contains a selection of the best primary songs. It is suited to primary or intermediate schools and to ungraded schools. The sentiments are excellent, and the music attractive. It has Opening Songs, Songs for all the Seasons, Welcome Songs, Nature Songs, etc., etc. There should be a few minutes of singing daily in every school. This book is so inexpensive that you can easily supply your class with it.

15 Cts. a copy; $1.50 a dozen. Special prices quoted on larger quantities.

No. 2. Autobiography of Frœbel.

Materials to Aid a Comprehension of the Works of the Founder of the Kindergarten. 16mo, large, clear type, 128 pp. Unique paper cover. Price, 30 cents ; *to teachers,* 24 cents ; by mail, 3 cents extra. Bound in limp cloth, 50 cents ; *to teachers,* 40 cents ; by mail, 5 cents extra.

This little volume will be welcomed by all who want to get a good idea of Frœbel and the kindergarten.

FRIEDRICH FRŒBEL.

1. The dates connected with Frœbel and the kindergarten are given, then follows his autobiography. To this is added Joseph Payne's estimate and portrayal of Frœbel, as well as a summary of Frœbel's own views.

2. In this volume the student of education finds materials for constructing, in an intelligent manner an estimate and comprehension of the kindergarten. The life of Frœbel, mainly by his own hand, is very helpful. In this we see the working of his mind when a youth ; he lets us see how he felt at being misunderstood, at being called a bad boy, and his pleasure when face to face with nature. Gradually we see there was crystallizing in him a comprehension of the means that would bring harmony and peace to the minds of young people.

3. The analysis of the powers of Frœbel will be of great aid. We see that there was a deep philosophy in this plain German man ; he was studying out a plan by which the usually wasted years of young children could be made productive. The volume will be of great value not only to every kindergartner, but to all who wish to understand the philosophy of mental development.

La. Journal of Education.—" An excellent little work.'

W. Va. School Journal.—" Will be of great value."

Educational Courant, Ky.—" Ought to have a very extensive circulation among the teachers of the country."

Educational Record, Can.—" Ought to be in the hands of every professional teacher."

KELLOGG'S
RECEPTION DAY SERIES

SIX NUMBERS.

A collection of Recitations, Declamations, Dialogs, Class Exercises, Memorial Days. Everything in these books can be used. No scenery required. For general school use it is the best collection published and the cheapest. Each contains 160 pages with strong and pretty cover. 20c. each. The set of 6 postpaid (nearly 1,000 pages) for only $1.00.

Here is a hint of what these books contain:

NO 1 CONTAINS

29 Recitations.
14 Declamations.
24 Selections for Primary Classes.
25 Dialogs, among which are: "Christmas," for 9 boys and 6 girls. "The American Flag." for 8 boys. "A Stitch in Time Saves Nine," for 8 girls. "The Happy Family," for 2 girls and 2 boys "Who Shall Vote?" for 19 boys.

NO. 2 CONTAINS

29 Recitations.
12 Declamations.
24 Primary Pieces.
4 Memorial Day Programs for Garfield, Grant, Mrs. Sigourney, Whittier
4 Class Exercises -among them being Washington's Birthday, An Operetta, The Birds' Party, for Closing Exercises.
17 Dialogs.

NO. 3 CONTAINS

21 Recitations.
18 Declamations.
17 Primary Pieces.
22 Dialogs -among them these very popular ones: "Bob Sawyer's Evening Party," for 4 boys and 2 girls; "Work Conquers," for 11 girls and 6 boys. "Judging by Appearances," for 5 boys.

NO. 4 CONTAINS

21 Recitations.
23 Declamations.
5 Memorial Days—Thomas Campbell, Longfellow, Michael Angelo, Shakespeare, Washington.
7 Class Exercises, including one each for Christmas, Thanksgiving, Arbor Day, Tree Planting, Washington's Birthday.
8 Dialogs, including the very attractive Mother Goose's Party, for 2 girls and 4 boys.

NO. 5 CONTAINS

36 Recitations.
16 Declamations.
5 Class Exercises and Memorial Days as follows: Autumn Exercise —Mrs Browning Memorial Day— Bryant Memorial Day—Christmas Exercise—Tree Planting Exercises
21 Dialogs.

NO. 6 CONTAINS

41 Recitations.
6 Declamations.
4 School-Room Songs.
15 Primary Pieces.
6 Dialogs among them "Haw vs Hum." for 8 boys; "Choosing Vocations." for 2 boys and 3 girls.
10 Class Exercises, including "A Flower Exercise" (for little ones ; "A New Year's Greeting;" Holmes' Exercises; Our Nation's Birthday; Washington's Birthday Exercise.

Kellogg's Special Day Books—11 volumes—Price, 25c. each.

Kellogg's School Entertainment Series—17 volumes—Price 15 cents each.